KT-574-869

THE LITTLEST DRAGON GOES FOR GOAL

by Margaret Ryan

Illustrated by Jamie Smith

CollinsChildren'sBooks

An imprint of HarperCollinsPublishers

First published in Great Britain by Collins in 1999
Collins is an imprint of HarperCollins*Publishers* Ltd
77-85 Fulham Palace Road, Hammersmith,
London, W6 8JB

The HarperCollins website address is www.**fire**and**water**.com

3 5 7 9 8 6 4

Text copyright © Margaret Ryan 1999
Illustrations © Jamie Smith 1999

ISBN 0 00 675413 9

The author and illustrator assert the moral right
to be identified as the author and illustrator of the work.

Printed and bound in Great Britain by
Caledonian International Book Manufacturing Ltd,
Glasgow G64

Conditions of Sale
This book is sold subject to the condition
that it shall not, by way of trade or otherwise,
be lent, re-sold, hired out or otherwise circulated
without the publisher's prior consent in any form,
binding or cover other than that in which it is
published and without a similar condition
including this condition being imposed
on the subsequent purchaser.

THE LITTLEST DRAGON
GOES FOR GOAL

Collins
YELLOW
STORYBOOK

CONTENTS

HAPPY BIRTHDAY,
LITTLEST DRAGON!

It was a very special day. In the
dragons' cave, ten dragons lay in the
big dragons' bed. Nine of the dragons
were fast asleep, but the littlest one,
Number Ten, was wide awake.

"I wonder what the postman will
bring me today," he said, and jumped
out of bed to see.

"Happy Birthday, Number Ten,"
said the postman. "Here are all your
cards and parcels. Have a nice day!"

"I will," said the littlest dragon.
"My cousin, Emerald, is coming over
soon. We're going to play with all my
presents."

"I'm here already," yelled Emerald,
bumping up the path on her bike.
"Happy birthday, Number Ten.
Look what I got you!"

"Chocolate toffees. Yummy!" said Number Ten. "Thanks, Em. We'll eat these now, then we can watch my new football video and play my new computer game."

The littlest dragon opened up the box of chocolate toffees and was just about to reach in when...

"I thought I could smell chocolate toffees," said big dragon brother, Number One.

"I can always sniff out chocolate toffees," said big dragon brother, Number Two.

"So can we," said all the other dragon brothers, and grabbed the box.

"But they're MY toffees," said Number Ten. "I got them for MY birthday."

"Remember to share," laughed all the dragon brothers and started to eat the sweets.

By the time the littlest dragon got the
box back, only the wrappers were left.

"This won't do," muttered the
littlest dragon. "This won't do at all."

Then he had his first idea.

"Come on, Emerald," he whispered. "We'll go and watch my new football video while they're busy munching."

The littlest dragon put on the video and he and Emerald were just about to watch it when...

"A new football video. Brilliant," said big dragon brother, Number Four.

"We love football videos," said twins, Five and Six.

"Shove along, Number Ten, so we can see," said big brothers One, Two and Three.

"But now Emerald and I can't see," said the littlest dragon, as they were pushed THUMP on to the floor, and elbowed OUCH to the back of the room. "And it's MY video. I got it for MY birthday."

"Remember to share," laughed all
the other dragon brothers, and jumped
up to cheer when a goal was scored.

"This won't do," muttered the
littlest dragon. "This won't do at all."

Then he had his second idea.

"Come on, Emerald," he whispered. "We'll go and play with my new computer game while they're busy watching."

The littlest dragon switched on the computer, loaded his game, and then he and Emerald began to play.

They were both just getting a really high score when...

"A new computer game. Cool," said big dragon brother, Number Nine.

"I love computer games," said big dragon brother, Number Three.

"Shove over, Number Ten, it's our turn next," said twin dragon brothers, Five and Six.

"But now Emerald and I can't play," said Number Ten, as they were pushed THUMP on to the floor, and elbowed OUCH to the back of the room. "And it's MY game. I got it for MY birthday."

"Remember to share," laughed all the other dragon brothers, and fought over who should be first to play.

The littlest dragon took Emerald's
hand and stomped into the big cave
kitchen.

"It's not fair," he muttered.

"What's not fair, Number Ten?" asked his mum, who was busy making his special birthday cake.

"It's not fair that we can't get to play with MY birthday presents on MY birthday. Just because we're the littlest."

Then his mum had an idea.

"Why don't you and Emerald mix up this birthday cake while I go and have a word with these big brothers," she said.

"Okay," said the littlest dragon.

Then he had his third and naughtiest idea.

"Come on Emerald," he whispered. "We'll mix salt into the cake instead of sugar while the others are busy playing."

"That's your best idea yet, Number Ten," giggled Emerald.

Soon the littlest dragon's mum came
back and popped the cake in the oven.

When it was ready, the littlest dragon
was just blowing out the candles
when...

"I thought I could smell birthday cake," said big dragon brother, Number One.

"I can always sniff out birthday cake," said big brother, Number Two.

"So can we," said all the other dragon brothers, and cut themselves such huge slices that there was none left for the littlest dragon or Emerald.

"What about us?" asked the littlest dragon. "It's MY cake. It was made for MY birthday."

"Remember to share," laughed all the dragon brothers, and took enormous bites of the cake.

"EEK ARRRGH OOH YUK!!!!"
they all yelled, and ran outside
holding their throats and their tums.

"Oh dear," said their mum. "I'm always telling them not to be so greedy. Never mind, Number Ten, I'll make you and Emerald another little cake. Here are some chocolate toffees to keep you going till the cake's ready."

"Thanks, Mum," said the littlest dragon, and he shared the toffees with Emerald.

"We'll eat these now," he grinned. "Then we can watch my new football video and play my new computer game!"

THE LITTLEST DRAGON
GOES FOR GOAL

It was Saturday afternoon. In the dragons' cave, the ten dragon brothers were getting ready to go to the next field to watch their favourite football star, Dragon McFeet, play his weekly game.

"I'm wearing the special winning jersey Dragon McFeet gave me," said the littlest dragon. "Pity I've only got these old boots of Number Nine's."

He was just lacing up the old boots when his nine dragon brothers thundered past him on their way to the game.

"Wait for me," yelled the littlest dragon, tripping over his laces.

The dragon brothers found a good spot behind the goal, and clapped and cheered as Dragon McFeet scored the winning goal.

Then Dragon McFeet made a special announcement.

"At next week's game," he said, "my boots will be raffled to raise money for the Baby Dragons' Hospital. I hope you will all buy a ticket."

"We will," said dragon brothers,
One and Two.
"Yes, yes," said Three and Four.

"We'll run home right now and
empty our dragon banks," said twin
dragon brothers, Five and Six.

"Wait for me," cried the littlest dragon, as nine dragon brothers thundered past him back to the dragons' cave.

The littlest dragon tripped along behind. But when he got home, his brothers were looking miserable.

"My dragon bank's empty," said Number Eight.

"I've only got a button left," said Number Seven.

"I found a hairy toffee in mine," said Number Two.

The littlest dragon smiled and got out his dragon bank.

"There's still some birthday money in mine," he said.

But there wasn't. Instead there were some letters which said...

Dear Number Ten,

I borrowed some money for football stickers. Will pay you back soon.

Love,

Number Three.

Dear Number Ten,

I borrowed some money for lollipops. will pay you back soon.

Love,

Number Nine.

Dear Number Ten,

we borrowed some money for dribbly chocolate ice cream. we love dribbly chocolate ice cream. will pay you back soon.

Love,

the twins (Five and Six).

"Oh no," said the littlest dragon. "How will I be able to buy a raffle ticket for Dragon McFeet's boots?"

Then he had his first idea.
"I'll go and ask Mum if she needs
any jobs done in the house," he said.
"That way I can earn some money to
buy a raffle ticket."

"Good idea, Number Ten," said his nine dragon brothers, and thundered past him into the kitchen.

"Wait for me," cried the littlest dragon. "It was MY idea."

But by the time he got to ask his
mum what he could do to earn some
money, there was only cleaning the
smelly wellies left.

"I hate cleaning the smelly wellies,"
said Number Ten. "Why do dragons
have such smelly feet?"

The dragon brothers' smelly wellies were kept outside the back door, so the littlest dragon picked up the garden hose and scooted them with water.

Then he went back into the kitchen.

"Any more jobs, Mum?"

"No, that's all," said his mum, and gave him some money.

But he still didn't have enough to buy a raffle ticket.

Then he had his second idea.

"I'll go and ask Dad if he needs any jobs done in the garden," he said.

"Good idea, Number Ten," said his nine dragon brothers, and thundered past him into the garden.

"Wait for me," cried the littlest dragon. "It was MY idea."

But by the time he got to ask his dad what he could do to earn some money, there was only the muck spreading left.

"I hate muck spreading," said Number Ten. "Why do flowers need such smelly stuff to make them grow?"

He got out his red plastic spade from the cupboard in the hall, and huffed and puffed till he had covered the flower beds in muck. Then the littlest dragon's dad gave all the dragons the money they had earned.

"Wait for me," yelled the littlest dragon as his nine dragon brothers thundered past him on their way to the shop to buy their raffle tickets.

The littlest dragon tripped along behind, and got the very last one.

He couldn't wait for Saturday to arrive. As usual, the dragon brothers went to the game in the next field. They saw Dragon McFeet score the winning goal.

Then, when the game was over,
Dragon McFeet picked out the
winning raffle ticket.

"It's number... ten," he said.

"That's mine, that's mine!" cried
the littlest dragon, and he ran out on
to the field to get his prize.

He wore Dragon McFeet's winning boots, which were far too big for him, all the way home.

Next day, the dragon brothers went out to play their usual game of football. The littlest dragon wore the winning boots, but, every time he kicked the ball, the boots flew into the air too.

"Those boots are far too big for you,
Number Ten," said Number One.
"Better let me wear them."

"No, me," said Number Two. "I'm
sure they're my size."

"What about me, and me, and me?"
said the other dragons.

But then the littlest dragon had his third and smelliest idea. He hung the boots round his neck, put clothes pegs on his nose, and went and stood in the muck heap.

"If it can make the flowers grow," he squeaked, "perhaps it can do the same for my feet!"

THERE ARE MORE STORIES ABOUT THE
LITTLEST DRAGON WITH THE BIG IDEAS.

THE LITTLEST DRAGON
by Margaret Ryan and Jamie Smith

*It's hard being the youngest in the family, especially
when you've got nine older brothers!*

Find out how the
littlest dragon manages
to get a peaceful night's
sleep in the big
dragons' bed. And
then discover how he
manages to get a very
special winning football
jersey... for free!

Collins
An Imprint of HarperCollins*Publishers*
www.**fire**and**water**.com

THE LITTLEST DRAGON GETS THE GIGGLES
by Margaret Ryan and Jamie Smith

The littlest dragon is fed up. He wants to have the plastic frog from the cornflakes packet, but his big brothers always get there first. Then he wants to go swimming... but his brothers won't let him. But although he's the littlest dragon, he has the biggest and best ideas for getting his own way.

Collins

An Imprint of HarperCollins*Publishers*

www.**fire**and**water**.com

Order Form

To order direct from the publishers, just make a list of the titles you want and fill in the form below:

Name ....

Address ....

....

....

Send to: Dept 6, HarperCollins Publishers Ltd, Westerhill Road, Bishopbriggs, Glasgow G64 2QT.

Please enclose a cheque or postal order to the value of the cover price, plus:

UK & BFPO: Add £1.00 for the first book, and 25p per copy for each additional book ordered.

Overseas and Eire: Add £2.95 service charge. Books will be sent by surface mail but quotes for airmail despatch will be given on request.

A 24-hour telephone ordering service is available to holders of Visa, MasterCard, Amex or Switch cards on 0141- 772 2281.

Collins
An Imprint of HarperCollins*Publishers*